God,
Mrs. Muskrat
and Aunt Dot

Westminster Press books by ISABELLE HOLLAND

God, Mrs. Muskrat and Aunt Dot
Abbie's God Book

God,
Mrs. Muskrat
and Aunt Dot

by ISABELLE HOLLAND

Illustrated by
Beth and Joe Krush

THE WESTMINSTER PRESS
Philadelphia

Text copyright © 1983 by Isabelle Holland
Illustrations copyright © 1983 by Beth and Joe Krush

Book Design by Alice Derr

First edition

Published by The Westminster Press®
Philadelphia, Pennsylvania

PRINTED IN THE UNITED STATES OF AMERICA
9 8 7 6 5 4 3 2 1

Library of Congress Cataloging in Publication Data

Holland, Isabelle.
  God, Mrs. Muskrat, and Aunt Dot.

  SUMMARY: In a letter to God, recently orphaned
Rebecca explains how lonely she is now that she has gone
to live with her aunt and uncle and how helpful her
imaginary friend has been.
  [1. Orphans—Fiction] I. Krush, Beth, ill.
II. Krush, Joe, ill. III. Title.
PZ7.H7083Go 1983   [Fic]   82-23794
ISBN 0-664-32703-6

God,
Mrs. Muskrat
and Aunt Dot

7044161

Dear God:

I've decided to write you this letter because I don't have a best friend and I don't know anybody here.

I don't really know anybody anywhere else. An orphan being passed around among relatives does not have a permanent domicile—I learned that word in school today—domicile. It sounds domestic and cozy, like toasting muffins, not like the word "home," which has a long haunted sound, especially if you don't have one.

As you know, God, I am eleven. Daddy died when I was five. I don't really remember him—just a hole somewhere. Mother was an actress and would go on the road a lot. But she was a lot of fun. That is, she was before she got sick. She died last year, but she was pretty sick for a year before that. I was staying with Aunt Dot and Uncle Matthew at the time.

I was at school that day. In the middle of history class I suddenly knew Mother was dead. It's hard to

describe *how* I knew. The teacher called on me not long after that. I just sat and stared at her. She said I was recalcitrant. That's another word I learned. Then, in the afternoon, Miss Phelps, the principal's assistant, came for me. As we walked to the principal's office she kept saying how we must always be brave no matter what. When we got there Aunt Dot was with the principal. She said, "Now, I want you to prepare yourself for bad news." She looked awful.

I said, "It's all right. You don't have to break it to me gently. I know, Mother's dead."

"How did you know? Who told you?"

"An angel," I said, because it sounded nice.

"You dear child." She started to come towards me, but I backed away. I wanted to kick her. She smiles all the time and talks to me in a special voice. She says she loves children.

I hate grown-ups who say they love children. It makes me feel like a crowd.

In church on Sunday the minister said a prayer with the words "Lighten our darkness, we beseech thee, and by thy great mercy . . . something, something . . ."

I asked Aunt Dot why the preacher always talked about mercy. Why did we need so much mercy?

Aunt Dot said because we were always being wicked.

I said I hadn't been particularly wicked this week.

Aunt Dot said what about the time I had stolen

Percy, the neighbor's black Lab, and taken him for a run down by the river.

I said I didn't steal him, I borrowed him. And anyway, he needed a walk. And double anyway, my dog Sammy had been taken away from me when Mother got sick. He'd been taken by the pound, and as everybody knows, after three days, when nobody comes to claim them, the animals at the pound have to be killed.

Aunt Dot didn't say anything until after we crossed the main road. Then she said, "I suppose you blame me for that. Well, I can't help it, I won't have animals in the house. And there's no place in the yard to keep him."

Every time I think about Sammy, anger, like a cold snake inside me, starts to uncoil. Sammy was a sandy mutt with wavy hair and large ears. He had a beautiful soul. I've hated Aunt Dot and church and God ever since she said dogs didn't have souls.

I told her she was an old frump with the soul of a worm. And Sammy had a better soul than she did.

We didn't speak for about a week. Then when we went to church the preacher preached that animals did not have souls and were made for the use of man. The Bible said so. See Genesis. I knew Aunt Dot put him up to it.

That's when I gave up the Bible and church and God. (Sorry, God, I'd forgotten that when I started this letter.)

I can see now from what I wrote before that I sound crazy. I said I gave you up and then I wrote a letter to you.

That bothered me all day yesterday. I was talking to Mrs. Muskrat, who's a friend of mine. (I'll explain about her in a minute.) She said, "How can you give up God and then write him a letter?" It's the kind of question she always asks, and then I have to go off to my winter office and think. My winter office is that hole down by the lake under the embankment. Nobody knows it's there because of that big bush in front. I only discovered it because I thought I saw a kitten disappear there one day. Anyway, I went there and sat on the magic stone and thought. (The stone is like the Stone of Scone that's under the throne in Westminster Abbey. Without the Stone of Scone it isn't a proper throne and the monarch can't be crowned. I call my magic stone the Stone of Rebecca. I feel that any thought I have while sitting on the Stone of Rebecca is official and probably right.)

Anyway—I went to the Stone of Rebecca and thought about the two Gods.

The one I talk to and write to and think about is God I. Most times I think of him as Great Spirit, like the Indians. He's everywhere, but especially among trees. And sometimes if I move fast enough, or turn my head quickly, I can see him and he's like a Light. Only you have to be at the right angle, and you almost never are. Sometimes he's inside me. And

11

inside me so far that it's like going through a long tunnel, the longest in the world. And there he is—wise, kind, wanting the best for me, wanting me to do the right thing and always on my side.

That's the God I write to and talk to.

God II lives in Aunt Dot's church and he's the one I gave up.

Mrs. Muskrat is round and wears a large white apron. She lives in the kitchen in her house in The Forest and is always baking cookies. I started talking to her whenever I was in my winter or summer office (my summer office is a large oak near my winter office). Both offices are near the river, which is important. Mrs. Muskrat has to live by the river. She says she feels better there. Whenever I have a problem I tell her. Sometimes she says, "There, there." Sometimes, "Have a cookie." And sometimes, "It'll be better tomorrow. You'll see." Often she says all three. When Sammy went, she said, "You'll see him again when you go to Heaven. He'll be waiting there for you." Now I talk to her anywhere.

Once, when Aunt Dot was saying how Sammy would have got hair all over everything, I told her he was in Heaven. "No he isn't," Aunt Dot said.

"Yes he is."

"No he *isn't!* Don't argue with me. Animals don't go to Heaven."

"You're a liar," I said.

Aunt Dot and Uncle Matthew don't spank me. They believe corporal punishment is wrong. But

Aunt Dot told me how bad I was and how I had hurt her.

Mother used to spank me sometimes—if she was mad enough or I had pushed things a little far. But I never minded. I usually knew that I'd asked for it. She always hugged me afterwards and then we cried.

I told Mrs. Muskrat what had happened and how I had called Aunt Dot a liar.

"Have a cookie," Mrs. Muskrat said.

One day, when I was walking to school and talking to Mrs. Muskrat, Susan and Janey, two girls in my class, passed me.

"You're talking to yourself," Susan said.

"No I'm not."

"Yes you are. We heard you."

"I think you ought to see a doctor. You're hearing things," I said. "Always attack in defense," Uncle Wombat used to say. Uncle Wombat was the stage manager in one of the repertory groups my mother traveled with.

"It's you that ought to see a doctor, Rebecca Smith," Janey said. "You're an awful liar."

"I am *not*." I swung the books I had strapped together, and whacked her on the head.

Then of course I had to see the school counselor, the school psychologist, the principal, and Aunt Dot, who, for the umpteenth time, was sent for.

"You are incorrigible," Aunt Dot said when we were walking home.

"The school psychologist said I was deeply disturbed," I said proudly. It sounded important.

Aunt Dot looked at me. "Well, you don't have to feel so proud of yourself," she said. "It's not a compliment. It means you're bad." We walked a while. "How did it all start?" she asked.

"Janey Huston called me a liar. I won't take that from anybody."

"You called me a liar," Aunt Dot said. "Remember?"

"Well—you were. You said animals didn't go to Heaven. Sammy's in Heaven and it's because you put him there."

". . . eight, nine, ten," Aunt Dot said. "I'm counting ten so I won't lose my temper. I'm not going to argue with you about that anymore. But I *am* going to tell you that expressing a difference of opinion does *not* mean you're a liar. What made you call Janey a liar?"

I don't discuss Mrs. Muskrat with anyone. I started to once, when I thought someone was going to be best friends with me, but when I tried to talk to Mrs. Muskrat again, I couldn't find her. All I could see very faintly were her whiskers and her soft brown fur. No kitchen, no apron, no cookies. So I never mentioned her again to anyone, and then one day she was back.

"Oh, I'm so glad to see you," I said. "Where were you?"

"Around."

"Don't ever go away again!"

"Not until you don't look for me anymore."

15

"I'll always look for you! Always!"

"No," she said. "I'll always be a part of you. But you won't always look for me. One day you will find another human you like and then you will leave The Forest."

"Never."

"Yes. You will. But it won't feel like leaving. It will feel like finding someone else."

After that I was so frightened I'd lose her that I looked for her every day. And she seemed rounder and browner and warmer and dearer all the time. And she kept on baking more and more cookies. And the kitchen always smelled delicious.

But I wouldn't think of mentioning her to Aunt Dot.

"Janey said something that wasn't true. That's all," I said.

"*What* did she say?"

"No comment," I said, the way they do on TV.

"I just don't understand you at all," Aunt Dot said. "Your Uncle Matthew and I always wanted children and when we knew we weren't going to have any we were sad. Then, when Helen died, bad as that was, we thought we would have one—you. But we don't seem to get along very well, do we?"

"No," I said.

When things happen that I don't like I go into The Forest. I'm the only human allowed in it. It's filled with trees and leaves and burrows where all the animals live and God I lives there. He walks around, making sure everything is safe and no beasts or demons or humans enter the magic circle that he draws around The Forest every night. Sometimes God is a spirit and blows through the trees making a great long sound. Sammy lives there. He lives in the house with Mrs. Muskrat.

One day after the thing at school about whacking Janey Huston on the head, Aunt Dot took me to see someone downtown. We went into a house with an elevator and then into a room with a thick carpet.

"I'm going to leave you here now," Aunt Dot said. "But I'll be in another room down the hall, and I'll come and get you after a while."

Then she left. I sat there and looked around. There were chairs, a table with some magazines and a large mirror on the wall. It was terribly quiet.

I tried to think about Mrs. Muskrat, but The Forest seemed far away, on another planet. I looked at the magazines, but I didn't want to read one. I sat there, and was suddenly quite sure that somebody was watching me.

I closed my eyes and told myself no one was there.

But somebody felt there. I opened my eyes and looked around. Nobody. Only me, straight ahead, in the mirror. Ugly, as usual.

"You're not ugly," Mrs. Muskrat said. "I like skinny people with straight hair and no-colored eyes. They're like water, a clear brown, or maybe gray, or maybe both." And she gave me a whiskery kiss.

17

I got up and sat with my back to the mirror. "There's somebody there," I said very quietly to Mrs. Muskrat.

"I know."

"But do you know where it is?"

"No," Mrs. Muskrat whispered. "But you must be very quiet and brave and not give anything away to anyone."

"I won't," I promised.

The door opened. A large man with a lot of teeth came in.

"Hello," he said. "My name is Joe. What's your name?"

I checked quickly with Mrs. Muskrat. "It's all right. You can tell him your name," she said. "But nothing about The Forest."

"Where is God?" I asked Mrs. Muskrat.

"In the center of The Forest, with us. I must go now." And I knew I was alone.

"Aren't you going to tell me your name?" Joe said.

"Rebecca."

"Hello, Rebecca." His breath smelled. I decided Uncle Matthew was better than he was.

The large man sat down. "Why don't you sit on the sofa? It's much more comfortable."

"I'd rather sit here," I said.

"Lots of people like the sofa better," he said. "Why don't you like it?"

"I just don't."

"Is it because of the mirror?"

I wondered suddenly if he'd heard my conversa-

tion with Mrs. Muskrat. "What mirror?" I said.

He stared at me for a moment. "That big one over there." He waved towards it.

"Oh!" I said. "Oh, *that* one!" And then, because he was looking at me very closely, "I didn't notice it before."

I tried to think about Mrs. Muskrat in her kitchen. She was taking out some dough, very thin, and cutting it into round shapes. "These'll be done in a jiffy," she said. I decided to have a quick conversation with her in my mind and pretend Joe wasn't there.

"Where's Sammy?" I asked Mrs. Muskrat.

"He isn't here," she said.

"I thought he was with you."

"No. He visited me once. I thought he was going to stay, too. But he didn't. I expect he's with the Great Shepherd."

"What Great Shepherd?"

"The one who lives in the middle of The Forest."

"Have you ever been there?" I said.

"No. But he comes to see me sometimes."

"What does he look like?"

"Well, Sammy said he looked like a Great Shepherd. But it couldn't have been the same one, because when he was here he looked to me like a very big, very wonderful Muskrat."

"And he lives in the middle of The Forest?"

"Yes."

"I thought that was where God lived."

"That's who I'm talking about."

"What are you thinking about?" the large man in the small chair asked.

I glanced back at him. "About my dog, Sammy."

"What about Sammy?"

"Aunt Dot had him executed."

"But I thought—what she did was send him to the shelter."

"You know Aunt Dot?" I said.

"Yes, I've met her."

I thought about coming here, the room, Aunt Dot leaving me here, the mirror. It was just like a program I saw once on television.

"You're a psychiatrist," I said. "And that's one of those mirrors you can see through from the other side. And she's there watching us! I think that's mean and unfair. How would you like it if I did it to you?"

And then I almost did a terrible thing. I almost mentioned Mrs. Muskrat. I nearly said out loud, "Mrs. Muskrat was right. She told me not to say anything."

For a terrible minute I wondered if he could see Mrs. Muskrat in my mind as she slid the cookie sheet into the oven. To make sure he couldn't, I turned around and said into the mirror, "I know you're watching me, Aunt Dot. How would you like it if I brought you here and stuck you in a room and watched you?"

There was a silence. Then the door opened, and Aunt Dot came in.

"I was just trying to help you," Aunt Dot said.

"You yourself told me the school psychologist said you were deeply disturbed."

"Yes, he did, didn't he?"

"And furthermore, you're proud of it."

"Rebecca Smith," I said, seeing the words on a plaque in my mind. "D.D. Deeply Disturbed." And then giggled. "Just like the preacher."

And then Aunt Dot surprised me. She laughed too.

"I don't like this room. Let's go," I said.

"I don't like it either," Aunt Dot replied. "Come on."

"But—" the large man said as we went to the door.

"Send me a bill," Aunt Dot called, as we went down the hall. "The school psychologist thought I should bring you here. The one that gave you the title you're so proud of. He said you had trouble with social relationships."

"What are those?"

"People," Aunt Dot said gloomily.

And then I met a people I liked. Her name was Mrs. Mushroom.

She lived in a falling-down shed at the edge of town, and her thirteen cats lived in the shed with her and in the garden around her.

"Actually," Mrs. Mushroom said, "this was once a sort of gardener's shack at the edge of a large estate. Only the big house was torn down. Then the roof of the shed fell in, so I found this useful box—a grand piano came in it once—and dragged it here, and it makes a very good roof. It's cozy, don't you think?"

I looked around. It really was a box overhead and not a proper roof.

"See?" Mrs. Mushroom said, pointing to the ceiling. I looked up and read the words, "Bronson Piano Company."

"This was one of their largest pianos," Mrs. Mushroom said proudly. She took out a small pipe and started smoking it. I must have looked shocked, because she took it out of her mouth and said, "Takes away the smell."

There *was* a powerful smell, of a great number of cats and of Mrs. Mushroom herself. It was funny, I thought, the way I minded the way the psychiatrist's breath smelled, but not at all the way Mrs. Mushroom and the cats smelled. Besides, the pipe did take away the smell. Grown-ups wouldn't like it, but, then, they probably wouldn't like anything about Mrs. Mushroom.

"Where do you sleep?" I asked.

"There." She pointed with her pipe to a corner. The wall of the old shed came higher there than anywhere else and there was part of the old wooden floor left. Besides, a plastic tarp was spread on top of it and there were layers of newspapers and on them a quilt, a woolen rug and some woolly scarves. "Cozy," she said again. It looked especially warm because right at that moment it was covered with cats.

"What are their names?" I asked.

THIS SIDE UP

Mrs. Mushroom and I were sitting on small wooden boxes around a sort of fire built at the other end of the house where there was a hole in the roof.

"Well," she said. "The ones there are Allegra, Constantine, Augustine, Hildebrand, Cleopatra, Boadicea, Queen Elizabeth I and George III. He's the one that's always losing things."

I had come home from school a different way because I knew Janey Huston and her gang were waiting for me on the usual route. So I ducked down a side road and got into the country and after that it seemed easy to go over a hill and into the area around a quarry. No kids were allowed there because the quarry had holes. Mrs. Mushroom's house was not far from the quarry.

"I like it here," she said. "Nobody comes because a couple of people were killed falling down the hole."

"Aren't you afraid?" I asked.

"Of falling down the hole?"

"No." What I was going to say was the kind of thing I could say to Mrs. Muskrat but usually to no one else. But I said it to Mrs. Mushroom. "Of ghosts."

"Oh! Ghosts. Of course not. They're very friendly. We talk all the time. You know," she said, taking the pipe out of her mouth, "I don't have a watch. Don't need it. But it's getting late. Your family'll start sending out search parties. And I don't want any search here. So you'd better go home."

I stood up. "All right. Can I come back?"

"Sure. But don't go chattering about it. People'd

28

come and the cats wouldn't like it. Me neither. See you."

"Where've you been, Rebecca?" Aunt Dot asked. I could smell that she'd burnt the dinner. But even burnt it tasted delicious, I was hungry.

"I took a walk," I said between mouthfuls.

"A walk! You're hours late. I was frantic. Where did you go?"

"In the country."

"Near the quarry?"

"No. In the opposite direction."

"Were you by yourself?"

"Absolutely," I said.

"You mean you went for a three-hour walk in the country until after dark, all alone?"

I decided it would sound better if I weren't.

"Except for Jonesey."

"Who's Jonesey?"

"A boy from school."

Aunt Dot looked deeply suspicious. "You never mentioned him before."

"He hadn't come up in the conversation," I said very casually.

"Jonesey who?"

"Jones."

"*What* Jones?"

"Jonesey."

"What's his *real* name?" Aunt Dot sounded exasperated.

"I just told you. I've finished dinner now. May I go to my room?"

"Not until you tell me who this Jonesey is."

"I just told you and you weren't listening, Aunt Dot. You're always telling me I don't listen. Well, you don't either." And I left the room quickly but with dignity.

That night I lay in bed and thought about Jonesey.

"You know," Mrs. Muskrat said, "lying is not a good idea."

"Why not? If people ask nosey questions and have to have an answer, what else can you do?"

Mrs. Muskrat didn't say anything at all. She was busy putting cookies in a jar.

"What would you do?" I asked. "You know Mrs. Mushroom said I shouldn't mention her."

Mrs. Muskrat put the lid on the cookie jar. "Well, there's the practical problem: You might get caught. Suppose Aunt Dot went to your school and demanded to see Jonesey. What would happen?"

Immediately I saw in my mind Martin Jones, president of his class, editor of the school paper, and captain of the baseball team. Mr. Perfect. Blond, blue eyes, terrific. He even has a dog who looks a little like Sammy. Golden, he's called, because he's a golden retriever. Every day when school's out Golden is waiting at the school entrance. Then he and Jonesey run home, or run to the athletic fields, or just run.

One day Golden came over and sniffed at the hand I held out. I hadn't eaten all my sandwich for lunch, so when I saw Golden I broke off a piece of roast beef Aunt Dot had put in the sandwich, just the way I used to offer a piece of my sandwich to Sammy, and offered it to Golden. Golden was about to take it when Jonesey called, "Golden, come here. I've told you *never* to take anything from strangers."

Golden trotted back.

"Bad dog," Jonesey said. "Sit."

Golden sat.

"I'm not a stranger," I said.

"Sure you are. Come on, Golden, let's run."

And they ran down the road and through the park, and I still had the beef in my hand.

"Hi," I said to Jonesey the next day.

"Hi," he said, and walked past and talked to Janey Huston, who's very pretty.

I didn't want Aunt Dot to find out about Jonesey and Golden.

The next morning Aunt Dot looked at me over her toast.

"I think you made up this Jonesey character."

I didn't say anything.

"I could call the school and find out," she said.

I said to Mrs. Muskrat, whom I suddenly saw very clearly in my mind, putting a sheet of cookies into the oven, "Now what shall I say?"

"Well," Mrs. Muskrat said, rolling out some more dough, "you seem to have got yourself in some kind of a bind. You can't say Jonesey's real, because Aunt Dot might go and talk to him. But you can't say he isn't real."

"Why not?"

"You figure it out."

Mrs. Muskrat took off her apron, put on a scarf and started to leave.

"Where are you going?" I said, alarmed.

"I'm going out for a walk in The Forest. I'm going to see the Great Muskrat."

"But you said that the Great Muskrat looked like God."

"Did I say that? I thought I said that God looked like the Great Muskrat."

"Isn't that the same thing?"

"No, it isn't," Mrs. Muskrat said, and left.

"REBECCA!"

I jumped. Aunt Dot was staring at me. And then I got a nasty shock. For a minute—just a minute, I thought she looked like Mrs. Muskrat. I was so startled. I blurted out, "Do you know Mrs. Muskrat?"

"Who?"

And then I came to, and the two worlds split apart again. "Nothing," I said.

"I thought you said something about a muskrat," Aunt Dot said.

"Did I? I must have been thinking about Sammy."

"I don't see what that has to do with muskrats."

The way she said it made me furious, as though they were just animals.

At that point Uncle Matthew came in. "Good morning," he said. And then eyed his empty place. "Where's my coffee?" he said to Aunt Dot.

She got up. "I'm sorry. I forgot to put it on," she said.

"*You forgot my coffee?*" Uncle Matthew sounded as though he couldn't believe his ears.

"It's not the Alpha and the Omega," Aunt Dot said crossly, going into the kitchen.

"What are the Alpha and the Omega?" I asked Uncle Matthew. He's very old, at least forty. He has gray in his hair and always wears a gray suit. He also wears glasses. Now he took these off and I suddenly saw he had large, gentle brown eyes, rather like Sammy's.

"It's the first and last letters of the Greek alphabet," Uncle Matthew said, holding his glasses and wiping them with his handkerchief. "It's in the book of Revelation, the last book in the Bible. It means the beginning and the ending. In other words, the first and the last and everything in between." He paused and blew on his glasses. "I am the Alpha and the Omega," he said in a solemn voice.

"You are?"

"No. I'm quoting. God says that."

I suddenly saw the Great Muskrat. And before I could stop myself I said, "Do you think God looks like a Great Muskrat?"

Uncle Matthew stopped what he was doing and stared.

I wanted to kill myself. I had been incredibly

stupid and put Mrs. Muskrat and the whole Forest in danger.

I heard Aunt Dot coming towards the door into the dining room.

"No," Uncle Matthew said seriously. "But if I were a muskrat, then I'm quite sure that my image of God would be some great, cosmic muskrat."

Aunt Dot plunged into the dining room. "Here's your coffee," she said belligerently. Then she astonished me. She kissed him. I didn't think married people kissed. Only people in movies or on the stage or those in love.

I told Mrs. Mushroom what Uncle Matthew had said. We were sitting surrounded by Augustine, Hildebrand, Queen Elizabeth I and Macbeth. Boadicea was on Mrs. Mushroom's lap and Archimedes was on mine.

"That's interesting," Mrs. Mushroom said, when she heard about Uncle Matthew and the Great Muskrat. "You'd never know your Uncle Matthew was a banker."

"Are bankers bad?" I asked.

"Well," Mrs. Mushroom said, picking a burr out of Boadicea's long fur. "Depends what your experience of them has been. Mine hasn't been good."

"What did bankers do to you?" I asked.

"Took away my cottage."

"I think that's *wicked*," I said.

"Well, I do too. Then"—Mrs. Mushroom puffed away at her pipe—"there's their side, too. 'You've got to remember other people have a side, too,' Mr. Mushroom was always telling me."

"How could they have any side at all in taking away your house?"

"They seem to think that not paying the mortgage shows lack of cooperation."

"What's a mortgage?"

"That's what I really never understood. A young man from the bank came and tried to explain it to me and I probably should have listened. But Rudolf of Hapsburg didn't like him and expressed himself on the whole subject."

"Who is Rudolf?"

Mrs. Mushroom sighed. "He's dead, but he was a wonderful dog. Very loyal. And one of the loyal things he did was bite the banker."

"Maybe he deserved it."

"I thought that too, at the time. But he was really only doing his job."

"What happened to your house?" I asked.

"They sold it, and then it was sold again, and then it was torn down to make a shopping center."

"Do you wish you had it now?"

"No. I'd be right in the middle of town and the children wouldn't like it."

"What children?"

"Boadicea, George III, Elizabeth I, Augustine and the others."

"Oh," I said. "You like it here better."

"Quarries are much nicer. Very private."

That night in bed I talked to Mrs. Muskrat, but it was a little harder than usual. I kept almost going to sleep and The Forest seemed far away.

"Why are you so far away?" I asked. "Have you moved?"

"No, Rebecca. You did."

During recess I'd sit and watch Golden and Jonesey. More and more Golden reminded me of Sammy.

Jonesey made me think of all the heroes I'd read about. I thought he was quite beautiful, but he never spoke to me.

Last Sunday I sat in church and listened to the preacher talk about God II. He finished by saying we were all born in sin and couldn't get out without Grace.

"Who is Grace?" I asked Aunt Dot.

"Weren't you listening?" she asked, sounding cross.

"Yes, sort of." Actually I had been having a quick conversation with Mrs. Muskrat, and the preacher's voice went in and out like bad audio on TV or a radio.

"Grace is like a warm wind when you're cold," Uncle Matthew said.

Two nights later I had a dream about Sammy. He was wandering all over a dark field and was looking for me. He looked wet and scared and miserable and

I knew if he didn't find me soon he'd die. Then I woke
up. And I was already crying, because the tears were
coming down my cheeks.

"Oh Sammy!" I said. The thought of his being
unhappy and lost and hungry was unbearable. I
tried to make myself feel better by imagining him
with Mrs. Muskrat in The Forest, or with the Great
Shepherd.

"Why aren't I feeling better?" I said to Mrs.
Muskrat.

"I don't know," she said.

"Why isn't Sammy with you?" I asked.

"I don't know," she said. She looked as unhappy as
I felt, which had never happened before. And she
was just standing in the middle of her kitchen doing
nothing.

"If he was with the Great Shepherd, why don't you
see him?" I said.

"That's what baffles me, too."

"Why aren't you baking cookies?"

"I can't seem to remember where I left the dough."

"You've never been like this before," I said crossly.

"No," Mrs. Muskrat said, still standing in the
middle of the kitchen looking baffled.

"I think you're stupid," I said, and started to cry
again.

What I wanted was for her to find the dough and
start furiously baking cookies and to give me a
whiskery kiss.

But none of that happened. She just got dimmer
and dimmer and dimmer, and I finally went to sleep
without being able to get her back.

It was the first time that had happened and I felt terrible.

"What's the matter?" Aunt Dot said at breakfast.

"Nothing," I said. I stared down at my English muffin.

"Isn't your muffin all right?" Aunt Dot asked. She sounded anxious. I suddenly realized she'd never had English muffins before. She'd always had toast, but I had a vague memory of telling her I liked muffins.

"It's fine, thank you," I said, and made myself finish the muffin. "Thanks for buying muffins," I said. I was still trying to find Mrs. Muskrat, but I couldn't even locate The Forest.

Suddenly I felt Aunt Dot's hand on my shoulder. "Whatever it is that is making you sad," Aunt Dot said, "it will get better."

"Do you ever buy chocolate chip cookies?" I burst out.

"Never," Aunt Dot said. "I don't approve of sweets. Sugar's bad for you."

"Mrs. Muskrat doesn't—" I said, and stopped horrified. That's the second time I'd almost given her away.

"I'm sorry," I said to Mrs. Muskrat in my mind. But I still couldn't find her.

"Did you say something about a muskrat?" Aunt Dot asked.

"No."

She was looking at me hard. "Well, I could have

sworn you did. And what's more, that's the second time . . ."

That day I sat outside school and waited for Golden to come and pick up Jonesey. But Golden didn't come. Jonesey came out with a bunch of other kids, including Janey Huston, and left without Golden.

"Aren't you waiting for Golden?" I called after him.

They all turned. I wanted to crawl into a hole. But I had to know where Golden was.

"He's at the vet," Jonesey said.

"What business is it of yours?" Janey Huston said.

I stuck my tongue out at her. Jonesey laughed. "I'll tell Golden you asked," he said to me.

Janey looked furious.

I felt wonderful.

"Don't you like anyone at school?" Aunt Dot asked that evening when we were fixing dinner.

I'd gone by Mrs. Mushroom's house to see her, but she wasn't there. I went over to talk to the cats, but they weren't very friendly. One of them, I think it was George III, hissed at me. So I went home. I'd done all my homework and it had started to rain. So I was upstairs reading a book when Aunt Dot knocked and then poked her head in.

"Why don't you come down and help me fix dinner?"

"I'm busy reading," I said.

"All right." She disappeared. I went on reading. I was mad at Mrs. Mushroom for not being there when I wanted her. I was mad at Jonesey for being good-looking and liking Janey Huston. I was mad at Aunt Dot for sending Sammy away—I'd never forgive her for that. I was mad at everybody at school for not being friends with me. I was mad at Mrs. Muskrat for disappearing and being hard to reach. I was mad at Mother and Father for dying. I was mad at everybody except Sammy, and I was even a little mad at him for not being someplace in The Forest where I could see him.

"What's the matter?" Aunt Dot asked from the door.

"I'm mad at the whole world," I said.

"At *everybody?*"

"Everybody except Sammy—and you killed him."

There was a long silence.

Then Aunt Dot let out a sigh. "All right. You win. Sammy's not dead. He's living on a farm in the country. If you like, we can go out and get him."

"When?" I shrieked, leaping out of my chair.

"Now."

"Why did you tell me he was dead?" I asked Aunt Dot as we were driving out to the country.

"I didn't. You just decided that. I didn't want animals in the house," Aunt Dot sighed. "Hair and mess and muddy feet . . ."

"There's nothing wrong with mess," I said indignantly. "Mother lived in mess all the time. She said it was creative." Suddenly I had a vision of her makeup table in her dressing room at the theatre: powder, cake makeup, shadow, lipstick, and all kinds of mascara, combs, brushes, curling rods. A sense of sadness came over me, and I longed for the old days when Sammy and I would sit in her dressing room while I wrote a story or drew a picture. And we'd watch from the wings, and then Mother would come off stage and want to know if I'd done my homework. Homework was a sore subject. I liked history homework or reading homework, but I didn't like arithmetic or math. A couple of times . . . more than a couple of times . . . the school officer would come to see Mother and then there'd be a fight and Mother would promise to send me to school in the next town or hire a tutor. I had lots of tutors and hated all of them. In fact, I didn't like anybody except Mother, Mr. Wombat and members of the cast. Kids my own age were awful. They made fun of me because my ears stuck out and I was always two years behind, except in history and English.

"You're going to have to do something about that kid," Mr. Wombat would say to Mother every now and then, looking even gloomier than usual.

"I will, love," she'd always say.

Now it was later. I still hated school and all the kids still thought I was funny.

For a minute the picture of Jonesey slid across my mind. It was a picture that was sliding in and out of my mind more and more lately—especially just before I went to sleep. Sometimes he would come and take my book bag and he and Golden would walk home with me. Or they'd start to. Before very long, just as he was telling me how interesting he found me, Janey Huston would suddenly appear from nowhere. Jonesey would drop my book bag and they'd walk off together. It was very upsetting, and I'd try to go to sleep before that happened. But I was managing it less and less.

Having Sammy would make things different. I wouldn't need anyone, even Jonesey—even though he'd admire Sammy tremendously, and Sammy and Golden would be great friends and be a bond between us.

I could hardly wait to get to the farm. "Can't you drive faster?" I asked.

"No, I can't," Aunt Dot said. "I'm over the speed limit now."

Finally we got to the farm. I've liked all the farms I've read about in books, with ducks and chickens and goats and pigs and cats and cows, with the sun sinking and the barn a bright red.

But I didn't like this one. There were no animals—just a lot of fields with nothing growing in them.

"Where are the animals?" I asked, as we drove on the road between the fields.

"It's not that kind of farm."

I kept looking for Sammy as we got near the buildings. It had been months since he and I had been together, and I couldn't believe that he'd have been happy here.

"This is an awful place," I said to Aunt Dot. "Sammy must have hated it."

Aunt Dot didn't say anything for a minute. Then, "I didn't bring him here myself. A friend . . . a friend . . . who felt about animals the way you do, and didn't want him to go to the pound, told me about this farm. But she hadn't been to it either."

I didn't reply. I was too busy thinking about Sammy.

A cross-looking woman opened the door when we rang the bell.

"We came to get Sammy," Aunt Dot said. "We'll pay you, of course."

"Well, you can't. He's gone."

"Gone!" I almost yelled the word. I was terrified

she meant that Sammy was dead.

"Yes. Great guard dog he turned out to be. When any stranger came up he just wagged his tail. So when he slipped his rope and ran away we didn't cry. But you ought to pay me just the same," she said. "He ate plenty."

"Rope?" I said. I felt so terrible I thought I was going to be sick.

"Yeah. We kept him tied up!"

Suddenly in my mind I saw Sammy, sleeping in my bed beside me, waiting in Mother's dressing room while she was on stage. Always with me. And all these months tied up . . .

"You are an evil woman," I said. "I'm glad he ran away. Anything'd be better than being here."

"You keep a civil tongue in your head."

Aunt Dot said in a very quiet voice, "I agree with every word my niece says, and I feel just the way she does, only worse, because it's my fault Sammy was here."

"It's people like you ruin animals," the woman said. "They should be kept outside where they belong. They're meant to be of use. The Bible says—"

"Don't you dare quote the Bible to me," Aunt Dot said loudly. Then she stopped and started again. "If you should see him—Sammy—or find out where he is, let me know. Here's my card. I'll put my telephone number on it." And she scribbled rapidly. Then, as she handed the card to the woman, "There'll be a *reward*."

"How much?" the woman said.

"A large one," Aunt Dot said. "Come on, Rebecca."

We didn't talk for most of the way back. I was so unhappy I couldn't speak. I kept thinking of Sammy, lost, hungry, miserable. And I was furious at Aunt Dot. But every time I started to tell her how I felt I couldn't quite get it out because I could tell how badly she felt.

Then suddenly she said, "If you want to yell at me about letting Sammy go to such a place, you can. I deserve it."

I didn't say anything. I thought she deserved it, too.

"You can't yell at your aunt when she feels that rotten," Mrs. Muskrat said.

"I know now why you didn't see Sammy," I said to

Mrs. Muskrat. "He wasn't there. I mean, he wasn't with the Great Shepherd."

"No." She sounded as unhappy as I felt. "I'll pray to the Great Muskrat that he'll be all right," she said.

"You mean God I."

"Yes."

I prayed, too.

Uncle Matthew put an ad in the local paper describing Sammy and saying that anyone who found him and brought him to us would get a reward. Then he called the local pound to make sure they'd know who Sammy was if he showed up.

When I went to see Mrs. Mushroom I told her all about Sammy and the terrible farm.

"You never know," she said, "he might show up."

"I'll never forgive Aunt Dot," I said. "I was beginning to think she maybe wasn't so bad. But now—"

Mrs. Mushroom stroked Julius Caesar, who was on her lap. "If you don't forgive her, nothing's going to work."

"What do you mean? There're lots of people I've never forgiven."

"Who?"

"Well—Janey Huston for being mean, and Jonesey for not paying any attention to me and the other kids for making me feel like I have B.O. and Mother for dying just when things are going right, and Aunt Dot for taking Sammy away from me and putting him in that awful place, and . . . and . . ." Suddenly it

felt like it was raining and I had to blow my nose.

"Here." Mrs. Mushroom handed me a large handkerchief. "It's clean. I washed it in the river yesterday."

I blew my nose and wiped my eyes and saw that all the wet came from my eyes and not from the rain. "Thanks," I said.

"Forgiveness is a funny thing," Mrs. Mushroom said. "It does you more good than the people you forgive."

"Why?"

"I dunno. It's one of those funny laws. Maybe something to do with thinking and air waves and the Spirit."

"What spirit?"

"The one that's in everything and makes everything work. It's in you and me and the cats and your Sammy and the tree over there and the air in between. Only when you don't forgive you put some kind of a divider between you and the people you're not forgiving, and the Spirit doesn't get through. Hadn't you better go home? It's getting late. And the children and I don't want a bunch of people coming out here looking for you."

I didn't want to go home. I thought about Sammy all the time and kept remembering that it was because Aunt Dot wouldn't have him in the house that he was now lost.

"I don't want to go home," I said.

"Well then, go somewhere else," Mrs. Mushroom said. "I can feel all those unforgiving waves coming from you and they're making the cats and me nervous."

I left.

"I don't think that was very nice of Mrs. Mushroom," I said to Mrs. Muskrat, but she didn't seem to be listening. She was looking around her kitchen in a very bewildered way.

"You aren't listening to me," I said crossly.

"I can't find the dough for my cookies. I thought I had it all rolled out."

"Well, why don't you stop looking for the dough and listen to me, instead?" I asked. All of a sudden she faded away and was gone: there was no burrow, no kitchen, no dough, no cookie jar and no Mrs. Muskrat.

I went home because there was no other place to go to.

"Where've you been?" Aunt Dot asked me. "We've been terribly worried."

I looked over towards Uncle Matthew. Usually when Aunt Dot says they're both terribly worried, Uncle Matthew is reading the paper. But this time he actually looked worried. "I was seeing a friend," I said.

"Who?" they asked together.

"Nobody you know," I said. I could have kicked myself. Now they'd nose around until they found out about Mrs. Mushroom.

"Rebecca," Aunt Dot said. "It's past dinnertime. We've been waiting for you so we could eat. And you're telling us you've been seeing someone we don't even know. We can't let you get away with that. And if you think about it, you know we can't. I'm certainly not going to deprive you of food. So sit down and have your dinner. But after that I want you to go up to your room. And you're going to have to stay there until you tell us where you've been."

"I'm not hungry," I said. "I'll go up now."

There was a moment's silence. Aunt Dot's eyes were large and dark, so large it was almost as if she were holding them apart, as though . . . as though she were on the edge of tears. Uncle Matthew looked sad.

They're really nice people, I suddenly thought, going up to my room. Not wonderful like Mother and Uncle Wombat and the rest of the theatre troupe. Home then was Mother and Sammy and Uncle Wombat (his real name was something nobody could pronounce, but Wombat was like the first two syllables) and the special smell that seems to be in the back of all theatres everywhere and an excitement and hotels and motels and rooming houses. . . . But then there were the periods when I couldn't be with Mother and had to stay with a relative and go to school. Those periods were always awful. I hated all the schools because the kids always thought I was funny, but then I never stayed in one long enough to make friends. That was why Mrs. Muskrat was so important.

I concentrated hard to bring her back, thinking about her whiskers and apron and the dough rolled out on a board, and her paw as she held the round cookie cutter. . . .

But what I kept seeing in my mind was Sammy, and when I pushed him away I saw Jonesey and Golden. . . . But if I just gave in and thought about Jonesey, then what about Janey Huston?

For a long time I sat on my bed and thought about Janey Huston. No matter where I went there was always a Janey Huston, prettier than I am, friends with everyone, and always making me feel ugly and stupid.

"What am I going to do about Janey Huston?" I asked Mrs. Muskrat.

But Mrs. Muskrat wasn't there. The room was dark. There was no Sammy, no Mother, no Mrs. Muskrat, no God I, nothing—only God II and he didn't like me, and I didn't like him because he didn't like me and had nothing but rules . . .

There was a knock on the door.

"Come in," I said.

I knew it would be Aunt Dot and I resigned myself to having her try to reform me and try to make me like Janey Huston.

But it wasn't. It was Uncle Matthew, peeping around the door, looking very stiff in his business suit, with his short hair neatly combed and his glasses on his nose.

"May I come in?" he said. He sounded unsure.

"Yes." I would *rather* be alone, I told myself. But without Mrs. Muskrat it wasn't true. Suddenly I felt alone, really *really* alone. I'd never felt that before

... or had I? My mind went back to empty rooms, a school dormitory, some people I was living with once when Mother was on the road. . . . That was when Mrs. Muskrat had come out of her burrow one morning and I had followed her back in and discovered her in her kitchen with her apron on and with the dough rolled out and the cookie cutter in her paw, and we started talking about The Forest. . . . It was long, long ago, when Sammy was still a puppy, before God I and God II. . . .

"Don't cry," Uncle Matthew said, and sat down on the bed beside me. He took off his glasses and started to clean them with his handkerchief.

"Why not?" I asked. "Everything stinks."

"Like what?"

"Like Janey Huston and Jonesey and Golden and Sammy being lost and Mrs. Mushroom and Mrs. Muskrat." I stopped. "*I didn't mean* to mention you," I said to Mrs. Muskrat. But it didn't matter, because she wasn't there anyway.

"Mushroom . . . ," Uncle Matthew said slowly, still polishing his glasses.

I knew I shouldn't mention her either, because of Julius Caesar, Elizabeth I, Boadicea and the others. . . . Some snoop might find out about her house near the quarry and decide to build a supermarket. I didn't want to mention Sammy because he was lost, or Golden because he belonged to Jonesey, who didn't pay any attention to me, or Janey Huston because she was prettier . . . which certainly limited conversation.

"Mushroom . . . ," Uncle Matthew said again.

"That's not her real name," I said quickly.

"I thought it might not be. But it sounds like somebody I once knew. I'd like to meet her."

"She doesn't like bankers," I said quickly.

"Oh. Has she had a bad experience with one?"

"He took away her house."

"I see."

"And she doesn't want anyone taking away her house or her privacy just because they want to build something stupid like a supermarket."

"Ah."

I felt it was perfectly okay to say that because there were, after all, hundreds of supermarkets.

"About Sammy," Uncle Matthew said. "You could always say a prayer that he'll be found."

"Your God wouldn't listen. Every time I ever tried to pray to him I knew I was so wicked—I'd broken all his favorite rules—that he wouldn't listen."

"You've been listening to the wrong preachers again," Uncle Matthew said gloomily. "You should never do that. They don't know anything real about God."

"Well then, why are they up there every Sunday morning going through what Mr. Wombat called God's rule book?"

"I guess because that's what they're paid to do. It's a great pity. God says something special to them at some point, so they decide to go off to seminary to become preachers so they can tell us about that special something they received—a whisper, a whiff, a touch. But as far as I can make out, all they learn at seminary is how to divide whatever it was they received and put it in neat little drawers with labels like theology this and theology that. So they come back and spend most of the rest of their lives taking out those little drawers so we can admire them and then putting them back in. And we never learn what that something special was—at least not from them."

I thought that was the most sensible thing I'd heard in a long time. "Then why do you go to church?"

"Because if you don't pay too much attention to the preacher but just sit there with the other people, you can sometimes feel that Something."

"I don't think you like God II at all," I said.

There was a very friendly silence then.

"Who is God I?" Uncle Matthew asked.

"The Great Muskrat," I said dreamily, not thinking. "Also, sometimes the Great Shepherd."

There was another even longer silence. I was trying to get back into communication with Mrs. Muskrat and it was beginning to feel as though I might do it.

"The Great Muskrat," Uncle Matthew said. "And/or the Great Shepherd . . ."

I was in a pleasant, sort of dreamy state. Suddenly I saw The Forest again, and Uncle Matthew and I were walking slowly under the trees. The funny part was, even though Uncle Matthew was dressed like a banker in his suit with a vest, he didn't look at all strange.

"You'll like The Forest," I said.

"Did you ever read a book called *The Wind in the Willows*?" he asked.

"No. Mother mentioned it sometimes and I was going to get it for a birthday but something happened."

"Well, there's a chapter in there. It's called 'The Piper at the Gates of Dawn.' I have a feeling," Uncle Matthew went on slowly, "that 'the Piper' might be another name for the Great Muskrat or the Great Shepherd. Why Muskrat?"

"Because of Mrs. Muskrat," I said. And all of a sudden I saw her quite clearly. She was busily cutting up the dough with her cookie cutter.

"My goodness," she said, "you have been away a long time. Who is that nice man?"

It was funny. Never before had I been able to see Mrs. Muskrat and a person at the same time in the same dimension. But there they were.

"Tell me about Mrs. Muskrat," Uncle Matthew said.

And not believing what I was doing, I did.

"That's interesting," Uncle Matthew said. "I wonder if she knows Crispin."

"Who is Crispin?"

"A dragon I knew when I was a boy. I grew up on a farm outside of town. And there weren't any other kids around. Anyway, I was in the field one day, supposed to be picking raspberries, when I saw

Crispin, a fine dragon with green scales and red eyes. I know it sounds funny, red eyes don't strike most people as becoming or attractive. But they were very warm and nice and suited him."

"How big was he?" I asked.

"About as tall as me—as I was then. But the interesting thing is he changed size according to the way I felt. If I was very busy with farm affairs and other things at school, he got so small he barely came up to my knees, and was almost colorless. But when he and I were together alone and everything else seemed far away, then he was large, even taller than me. He became a very bright green and his eyes glowed like warm fires."

"I wonder if he knows Mrs. Muskrat. Could you ask him?"

"Well," Uncle Matthew said, and took off his glasses again. "You understand it's been a long while since he and I chatted." He glanced at me. Once again I noticed how gentle and brown his eyes were. "You know you have very nice eyes," I said. "Not a bit like a banker's."

Uncle Matthew stopped rubbing his glasses with his handkerchief. "Bankers aren't all that bad," he said. "They're like everybody else—some good, some bad."

"Mrs. Mushroom says they have only one word in their vocabulary."

"No."

"No? You mean she's wrong?"

"No, I mean I'll bet she thinks No is our favorite word."

"Isn't it?"

"No. Sometimes we say yes."

Suddenly I saw Mrs. Mushroom in my mind's eye. "You'd never say yes to her," I said sadly.

"How do you know?"

"Because . . . you just wouldn't."

"She's the lady who doesn't like bankers."

"Yes."

"Because she had a bad experience with one."

"Yes. But Rudolf of Hapsburg took care of that."

Uncle Matthew put his glasses on again and looked at me through them. He looked more like a banker with his glasses on, of course, but this time I could see his brown eyes behind.

"Rudolf?" he said.

"Yes. A very loyal dog that Mrs. Mushroom had."

"And he bit the banker."

"Yes."

There was another friendly silence. Then Uncle Matthew said, "I had to go and see a funny elderly lady once. She hadn't been making her mortgage payments and the bank was threatening to foreclose."

"What does that mean?"

"It means take away her house. I went to see her and was in the midst of explaining what we might be able to do when the largest, shaggiest dog I ever saw came bounding into the room and bit me."

"Did it hurt?"

"Yes. And it hurt my feelings almost as much because the lady—her name was Munsion—said I deserved it for being a banker."

We didn't say anything for a while. Part of me felt terrible because I thought—now I've given away Mrs. Mushroom (I was sure she was Mrs. Munsion) and part of me thought it couldn't be too bad because Uncle Matthew had nice brown eyes and a green dragon for a friend.

"What ever happened to Crispin?" I asked.

"I'm not sure," Uncle Matthew said. "I guess what happened was that I grew up."

A great sadness filled me. "You mean people like Crispin and Mrs. Muskrat die when we grow up?"

"I don't think they die exactly. I think they go off and live in other dimensions."

"Oh. Can we ever see them again?"

"I don't know. I suppose if we really want to we can. But you know, Rebecca, it's hard to live in two dimensions at once. Unless, of course, where they kind of go together like space and time."

"You mean nobody can ever have friends like Mrs. Muskrat and friends like . . . like . . . Jonesey . . . at the same time."

"Not usually. A few sometimes do. Like some poets. But not often, and it's not comfortable for them."

"Why?"

"Well . . . , if you have Mrs. Muskrat, being friends with people like your friend Jonesey doesn't seem as important."

"Jonesey likes Janey Huston better anyway. And they all think I'm funny."

There was another silence. "Who did you say Jonesey was?" Uncle Matthew said.

I sighed. "Martin Jones. Mr. Perfect."

"What are you two doing up there?" Aunt Dot's voice floated up.

"Just chatting," Uncle Matthew said, getting up. "You know," he said, "your Aunt Dot isn't good at understanding about people like Mrs. Muskrat and Crispin. But she's terrific at coping with difficult problems like Jonesey and Janey Huston."

But you don't just go smack up to people and say, "I think Jonesey's terrific but he likes Janey Huston better and anyway she's prettier." So I didn't say anything to Aunt Dot. But that night something funny happened. I dreamed about Crispin. It started out to be a bad dream. I was walking in a nice green field which led to The Forest. But the road kept twisting and turning and every time I caught sight of The Forest it kept getting farther away. And it was also getting darker. Then suddenly it got lighter again and I could feel the sun, and I realized the reason it was darker before was because someone was standing in front of the sun and casting a shadow.

"Whoever you are," I said crossly, "I don't think you ought to stand in the sun and put people in the shadow." Then I looked up and there was this huge green dragon with warm red eyes standing beside me.

"You're Crispin," I said.

"That's right," he said. "Matthew Crispin, that's my full name. And there's no reason to be afraid."

"I'm *not* afraid," I said.

"Aren't you? I thought you were." And the red eyes, which were high above my head, looked down on me. They were so warm and kind they were like two little suns. And suddenly I remembered Uncle Matthew saying Grace is like a warm wind when you're cold.

"Do you know Grace?" I asked Crispin.

"Very well. Let's walk, shall we?"

So we walked a while in the warm sun across the bright-green hill. But when I looked up I couldn't see The Forest anywhere.

"Where's The Forest?" I said.

"Over there." Crispin waved his paw. "On the other side of those hills."

"But I'm trying to go to The Forest."

"No, you're not. We're going here." And the paw pointed to the edge of the hill.

I ran up the hill but when I got there I stood, shivering. Because it wasn't the edge of the hill, it was a cliff. And far below were the town and the school and Aunt Dot and Uncle Matthew and Jones- ey and Golden and somebody else I couldn't see clearly.

"But where's Mrs. Muskrat?"

"She's busy right now. But she told me to tell you

that it's not as bad as you think it is."

"What?"

"Flying off the edge of the cliff."

"What do you mean—flying off the edge of the cliff? Who's going to do that?"

"We are."

Fear, like a dark wet cloud, surrounded me. "No," I said.

"It won't hurt anywhere near as much as you think it will."

"I won't do it."

Suddenly I saw that what I thought was a cliff was really an immensely high stage, and all those people far below—Jonesey and Aunt Dot and Golden and the others—were the audience.

"But I belong in the theatre," I said. "Mother was there."

"Not now," Crispin said. "Anyway, how can you be in the theatre if you don't know anything about people? That's what the theatre is about—people."

"They all hate me," I said.

"No, they don't. Take my hand, we're going to *fly*."

Suddenly I found my hand inside the dragon's warm strong paw.

"Now," the dragon said. "I'm going to spread my wings. They're quite large, but you mustn't be afraid."

"I don't see any wings." I looked all over Crispin. The scales on his back were so green they glistened like green stars. But I couldn't see wings anywhere.

"All set?" Crispin asked.

"No."

"Try saying yes, just for practice. It'll get easier. Think of Sammy."

"Sammy—he's lost."

"But he's down there, isn't he?"

"Yes."

"You see, it wasn't hard to say yes."

And then suddenly Crispin's back started coming off. "Your back!" I cried.

"It's all right. Those are just my wings." And I saw they were. They kept unfolding and spreading until they were the size of the sky.

"Now, come on, jump," Crispin said.

I did, and he and I were flying, floating and gliding down, down, down, down. And there watching us were Jonesey and Golden and Aunt Dot and Janey Huston and the school, and . . . and . . . and I couldn't believe my eyes. Shaggy tail wagging furiously—there was Sammy.

"Wake up, Rebecca," Aunt Dot called.

I sat up in bed.

"Rebecca?" Her voice came from the foot of the stairs. "Now hurry up. You have to get to school."

"I don't want to go to school."

"It doesn't matter whether you do or not. You have to go. But first you have to look at something I have here." Something unpleasant, I thought.

I dressed slowly and went downstairs slowly. I felt strange and stiff—as though I had taken a long journey. I walked slowly into the kitchen.

And there was Sammy.

He was covered in dirt and mud which in a minute was all over my shirt and sweater because we were hugging each other and rolling on the floor and I was kissing him and he was licking my face.

"The shelter called this morning and said they had a dog answering Sammy's description, so your

Uncle Matthew went and got him."

"Please, can I keep him?" But I didn't have to ask. I knew I could.

"Of course." Then she sighed, stared at the wet paw prints and got out a mop. "We'll just all have to be patient," she said.

I jumped up and hugged Aunt Dot. Then Sammy jumped up and licked her. She looked as though she'd had a strange experience. Then she patted him. "Nice dog," she said.

I still didn't talk to anyone at school, but it didn't matter, because I'd come home straightaway and take Sammy for a walk.

One day I decided to stop by the quarry and see Mrs. Mushroom. I would have taken Sammy, but I didn't think Boadicea and the others would like it.

"You know," I said when I got there, "I think I know who that banker was. It was Uncle Matthew. He told me that he once got bitten by a dog when he was out to see somebody who was behind on the mortgage."

"I thought you might have something to do with it," Mrs. Mushroom said. "I asked him how he found me and he said he just kept investigating different ways of going from the school to his house and finally came this way." She puffed on her pipe for a minute. "I was pretty annoyed with you for jabbering about my private affairs that way until he said that people at the bank were feeling bad about me and they'd try and do something about a house."

"Uncle Matthew really is nice," I said. "He went

and got Sammy. And he once had a dragon friend called Crispin."

"Well, dragon or no dragon, I don't believe it's in the nature of banks to be warm and toasty. So I said where, figuring they'd want to move me. And I was right. They have some prejudice against the quarry here."

"So they're not going to build you a house?"

"We compromised. They're going to repair the floor, put in some kind of plumbing and build a ceiling. I guess your Uncle Matthew's not so bad." She looked at me. "How are you getting on with your forgiving?"

I thought about Janey Huston and how hateful she was. "Not very well. I still hate Janey Huston."

"Is she the only girl at your school?"

"No. They're dozens."

"Then why do you think about her all the time? How negative can you be? Who else is there?"

"There's Susan and Amanda and Anne and Francesca—"

"All in your class?"

"Yes."

"There you are. Think about some of those. But only think something nice. If you think anything not nice, they'll be not nice."

"That's silly."

"Try it. That's the trouble with you. You'd rather argue than try anything. What you need is a Friend. Capital F."

"I have Sammy."

"I'm sure Sammy is wonderful. But it's not the same."

"Also Uncle Matthew and Aunt Dot. They're okay. In fact, they're pretty nice."

"I said a *friend*."

"Like you."

"No. Not like me. Your age. A friend. F-R-I-E-N-D. People type. No tail, no fur, not grown up. Small, stubborn, ignorant, cowardly, but with dreams, like you."

"I'm not a coward."

"Prove it. Don't come back until you've done it. Now I want you to go. Elizabeth I wants to sit on my lap but she won't do it, until you go."

I was furious, and decided not to go and see Mrs. Mushroom anymore.

One day Aunt Dot was waiting for me after school with Sammy on his leash. "I thought you might want to walk him in the park," she said.

The next day Janey Huston said to me, "That's a pretty moth-eaten dog your aunt has. Not like Golden."

Jonesey was getting his books out of the locker nearby.

"Sammy is beautiful," I said, wishing I had something to hit her on the head with. "And you are a mean-faced witch to say that."

"Yeah," Jonesey said, slamming his locker. "That's one lousy thing to say about somebody's dog. I think he's neat and he looks smart."

"He is," I said. I was breathless with excitement. I couldn't believe Jonesey was talking to me.

"If you like that kind of mutt," Janey said, and walked off airily, her feet hardly touching the ground, pretending she didn't care.

Jonesey looked at me. "Wanna walk home? We could collect Golden and Sammy and take them to the park."

"Well," Aunt Dot said later, "how was your afternoon with Jonesey and his dog?"

"Terrific," I said.

Aunt Dot fussed around the kitchen for a while. I watched her and then nearly fell over when I saw what she was making. "Those are chocolate chip cookies," I said. "But I thought you didn't approve of them."

"I don't. But—well, I know you do."

I went over and hugged her and she gave me the bowl to lick. "There's nothing about chocolate chip cookies that I approve of," she said. "But . . . , sometimes you have to be flexible. By the way, I bumped into Mrs. Huston—Janey's mother—downtown. She's very worried about Janey."

"Janey's a toad. Except that I like toads."

"She says Janey needs friends but doesn't know how to make them."

"Making mean remarks about people's dogs isn't the best way."

"No. Mrs. Huston says that Janey always wanted a dog or a cat, but can't have one because she's allergic. She has a parakeet instead."

I was busy running my finger around the bowl and letting Sammy lick it, so I didn't say anything.

Two days later Sammy and I were walking to the grocery store when I bumped into Janey. We stood there, waiting for the light to change.

"My father says sometimes mutts are the smartest dogs," Janey said finally.

"What's your parakeet named?" I asked.

"Pico. When I go home I let it out of the cage and it sits on my head and grooms my eyebrows. Parakeets do that when they really like you."

"I'd like to meet him."

"Why don't you come home with me after school tomorrow?"

"Okay."

It was funny, but for a minute, I thought I saw, up in the sky, the outline of a huge dragon wing.

As Sammy and I walked home I thought about God I and God II, the Great Muskrat and the Great Shepherd and the whole Forest. And I thought about Aunt Dot and Uncle Matthew and Mrs. Mushroom and Jonesey and Golden and Janey. And then I finally thought about Crispin and Mrs. Muskrat . . .

They were all there. It was just that I couldn't see them all at the same time. They were there at different times in my life, but they were all there.

So you see, God, I now do know people and have a friend. In fact, I have two friends.

Yours respectfully,

Rebecca Smith